CHRISTMAS
TREASURY

ISBN 978-1-84322-666-6

1 3 5 7 9 10 8 6 4 2

Published by Armadillo Books
an imprint of Bookmart Limited
Registered Number 2372865
Trading as Bookmart Limited
Blaby Road Wigston
Leicester LE18 4SE

Produced for Bookmart Limited by Nicola Baxter
PO Box 215 Framingham Earl
Norwich NR14 7UR

Designer: Amanda Hawkes
Production designer: Amy Barton
Editors: Sally Delaney, Nicola Baxter
Illustrators: Pauline Siewert, Lucy Barnard

Material for this publication taken from *The Christmas Treasury* and
The Advent Calendar, both published by Bookmart Limited in 2006.

Printed in China

CHRISTMAS
TREASURY

Stories and Rhymes for a very Special Season

COMPILED BY NICOLA BAXTER AND SALLY DELANEY
ILLUSTRATED BY PAULINE SIEWERT AND LUCY BARNARD

CONTENTS

ARMADILLO

The First Noel

The first Noel the angels did say
Was to certain poor shepherds in fields as they lay;
In fields where they lay, keeping their sheep,
On a cold winter's night that was so deep.

Noel, Noel, Noel, Noel,
Born is the King of Israel!

They looked up and saw a star,
Shining in the east, beyond them far;
And to the earth it gave great light,
And so it continued both day and night.

And by the light of that same star,
Three wise men came from country far;
To seek for a king was their intent,
And to follow the star wherever it went.

This star drew nigh to the north-west;
O'er Bethlehem it took its rest,
And there it did both stop and stay
Right over the place where Jesus lay.

So let us all with one accord
Sing praises to our heavenly Lord,
That hath made heaven and earth of naught,
And with His blood mankind hath bought.

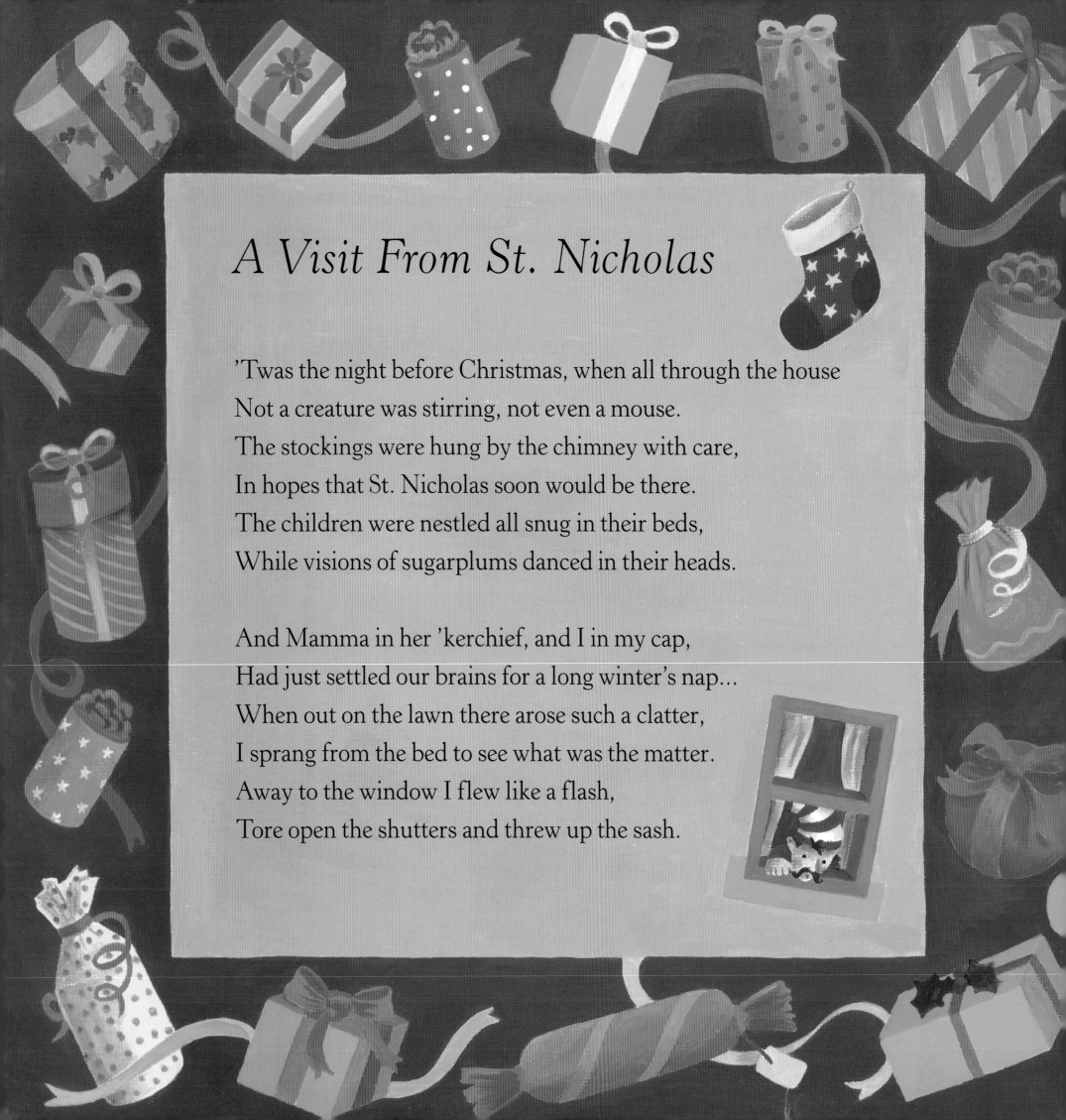

A Visit From St. Nicholas

'Twas the night before Christmas, when all through the house
Not a creature was stirring, not even a mouse.
The stockings were hung by the chimney with care,
In hopes that St. Nicholas soon would be there.
The children were nestled all snug in their beds,
While visions of sugarplums danced in their heads.

And Mamma in her 'kerchief, and I in my cap,
Had just settled our brains for a long winter's nap...
When out on the lawn there arose such a clatter,
I sprang from the bed to see what was the matter.
Away to the window I flew like a flash,
Tore open the shutters and threw up the sash.

The moon, on the breast of the new-fallen snow,
Gave the lustre of midday to objects below,
When what to my wondering eyes should appear,
But a miniature sleigh, and eight tiny reindeer,
With a little old driver, so lively and quick,
I knew in a moment it must be St. Nick.

More rapid than eagles his coursers they came,
And he whistled and shouted, and called them by name:
"Now, Dasher! now, Dancer! now, Prancer and Vixen!
On, Comet! on, Cupid! on, Donner and Blitzen!
To the top of the porch! to the top of the wall!
Now, dash away! dash away! dash away all!"

As dry leaves that before the wild hurricane fly,

When they meet with an obstacle, mount to the sky,

So up to the housetop the coursers they flew,

With the sleigh full of toys, and St. Nicholas, too.

And then, in a twinkling, I heard on the roof

The prancing and pawing of each little hoof.

As I drew in my head, and was turning around,

Down the chimney St. Nicholas came with a bound.

He was dressed all in fur, from his head to his foot,

And his clothes were all tarnished with ashes and soot.

A bundle of toys he had flung on his back,

And he looked like a pedlar just opening his pack.

His eyes—how they twinkled! His dimples, how merry!

His cheeks were like roses, his nose like a cherry!

He was chubby and plump, a right jolly old elf,

And I laughed, when I saw him, in spite of myself.

A wink of his eye and a twist of his head,

Soon gave me to know I had nothing to dread.

He spoke not a word, but went straight to his work,

And filled all the stockings; then turned with a jerk,

And laying his finger aside of his nose,

And giving a nod, up the chimney he rose.

He sprang to his sleigh,

   to his team gave a whistle,

And away they all flew

   like the down of a thistle.

But I heard him exclaim,

   'ere he drove out of sight,

"Happy Christmas to all,

   and to all a good night!"

Clement C. Moore

Jingle Bells

Dashing through the snow
In a one-horse open sleigh,
O'er the field we go,
Laughing all the way.
Bells on bobtail ring,
Making spirits bright.
What fun it is to laugh and sing
A sleighing song tonight!

Jingle, bells! Jingle, bells!
Jingle all the way!
Oh, what fun it is to ride
In a one-horse, open sleigh - hey!
Jingle, bells! Jingle, bells!
Jingle all the way!
Oh, what fun it is to ride
In a one-horse open sleigh!

You won't mind the cold,
The robe is thick and warm.
Snow falls on the road,
Silv'ring every form.
The woods are dark and still,
The horse is trotting fast,
He'll pull the sleigh around the hill
And home again at last.

We Wish You a Merry Christmas

We wish you a Merry Christmas,
We wish you a Merry Christmas,
We wish you a Merry Christmas
And a Happy New Year!

Glad tidings we bring
To you and your kin.
We wish you a Merry Christmas,
And a Happy New Year.

Oh, bring us some figgy pudding,
Oh, bring us some figgy pudding,
Oh, bring us some figgy pudding
And a glass of good cheer!

We won't go until we get some,
We won't go until we get some,
We won't go until we get some
So bring it right here!

We wish you a Merry Christmas,
We wish you a Merry Christmas,
We wish you a Merry Christmas
And a Happy New Year!

The First Christmas

One cold night, a little shepherd was watching his sheep on a hillside above Bethlehem. The sun set, and darkness came. The little shepherd looked up at the night sky. The stars were brighter than he had ever seen.

The sheep settled down, huddling together for warmth, and went to sleep. Around the fire, the grown-up shepherds sat and talked. The little shepherd felt his eyes beginning to close. He curled up next to a little lamb and began to dream.

While the stars slipped slowly across the sky, the little shepherd dreamed of warm food, and of running fast down hillsides, and of his mother and sisters safe at home.

Then it seemed to him as if a great, bright light shone all around him, and far away, someone was singing.

He opened his eyes and sat up. The sheep were sleeping. The fire was just a glow on the grass. But there was no one else to be seen. The little shepherd was alone.

He thought for a minute. He didn't like to leave the sheep, but he had a funny feeling there was somewhere else he should be. He picked up the lamb and set off to find the others.

He walked and walked, but the hills were dark and still.
At last, the boy turned towards Bethlehem, where a stable
huddled behind an inn on the edge of the town.

There, the little shepherd found the others.
He saw that they had found something too.
It wasn't a missing sheep. It was a baby!
Their faces were glowing with wonder
and happiness.

The little shepherd didn't know the baby was Jesus. He didn't know this was the very first Christmas Day. But he felt a happy, warm, excited, Christmassy feeling inside—and you know what that feels like, don't you?

The Perfect Christmas Tree

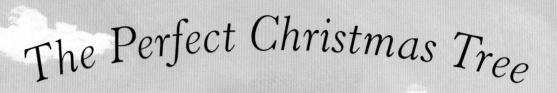

High on a windy hill, two trees grew tall and true. The sun smiled down on them during the day, and the moon turned their branches to silver at night.

One winter's day, a group of villagers climbed the hill, laughing and singing as they came. They carried spades and ropes and a huge picnic.

All day the villagers worked hard. At sunset, they finished their task. They had dug out the roots of one of the trees and carefully filled in the hole that was left. Then they dragged the tree down into the village.

That night, the tree that was left behind looked down the hill. Far below, a beautiful tree stood in the middle of the village, covered with lights and pretty things. The faint voices of grown-ups and children happily singing could just be heard.

The remaining tree stood still and alone until the sounds faded away. Slowly, something magical began to happen. High on the hilltop, sparkling snow started to fall, and stars dropped silently from the sky to twinkle on the tree's green branches. Little birds fluttered down to take their places. Then, as the tree stood dressed and ready to welcome Christmas Day, the birds opened their tiny beaks and sang, and creatures came from all around to their own perfect Christmas tree.

The Twelve Days of Christmas

On the first day of Christmas
My true love sent to me
A partridge in a pear tree.

On the second day of Christmas
My true love sent to me
Two turtle doves
And a partridge in a pear tree.

On the third day of Christmas
My true love sent to me
Three French hens.

On the fourth day of Christmas
My true love sent to me
Four calling birds.

On the fifth day of Christmas
My true love sent to me
Five gold rings.

On the sixth day of Christmas
My true love sent to me
Six geese a-laying.

On the seventh day of Christmas
My true love sent to me
Seven swans a-swimming.

On the eighth day of Christmas
My true love sent to me
Eight maids a-milking.

On the ninth day of Christmas
My true love sent to me
Nine ladies dancing.

On the tenth day of Christmas
My true love sent to me
Ten lords a-leaping.

On the eleventh day of Christmas
My true love sent to me
Eleven pipers piping.

On the twelfth day of Christmas
My true love sent to me
Twelve drummers drumming,
Eleven pipers piping,
Ten lords a-leaping,
Nine ladies dancing,
Eight maids a-milking,
Seven swans a-swimming,
Six geese a-laying,
Five gold rings,
Four calling birds,
Three French hens,
Two turtle doves
And a partridge in a pear tree.

Little Reindeer

Little Reindeer loved to play.
He liked to gallop away from
the herd as fast as his hoofs
would carry him…

then whirl around in a
flurry of snow…

and gallop even faster
back again…

before skidding to a dramatic stop
just in front of his mother.

"Now Little Reindeer," she would say,
"don't go too far away."

But Little Reindeer didn't listen.
One day, he ran so fast and far…

that when he whirled around, the herd was
nowhere to be seen.

He tried to follow his footsteps back to his mother,
but snow soon covered the marks.

Little Reindeer stood alone, feeling very, very sad.

At last, tired Little Reindeer fell asleep.

It was night when he opened his eyes again
and gasped with happiness. There was
his mother, smiling down at him.

"You found me!" cried Little Reindeer.

"Of course!" said his mother, "but you must promise me you will never run away again."

Suddenly, high above, there were other reindeer, flying across the sky. Behind them, a jolly man in red was dropping Christmas magic over everything!

A little bit of magic fell on the two reindeer below, and they trotted happily home for a very merry Christmas together.

O Christmas Tree!

O Christmas tree, O Christmas tree,
Your branches are so lovely.
Not only in the summer sun,
But when the winter cold has come.
O Christmas tree, O Christmas tree,
Your branches are so lovely.

O Christmas tree, O Christmas tree,
I love to see you standing here.
You fill us full of festive cheer,
Not only now but every year.
O Christmas tree, O Christmas tree,
I love to see you standing here.

O Christmas tree, O Christmas tree,
You show us how we ought to be.
You're strong and patient, standing tall,
You bring such happiness to all.
O Christmas tree, O Christmas tree,
You show us how we ought to be.